D0923157

Tobin, Paul, 1965-
Angry Birds comics. Fly
off the handle /
[2016]
33305243700519
gi 03/08/19

Cover Artwork by: Ciro Cangialosi

Edited for IDW by: David Hedgecock
Collection Edits by: Justin Eisinger & Alonzo Simon
Collection Production by: Chris Mowry
Publisher: Ted Adams

KAIKEN PUBLISHING LTD.

Laura Nevanlinna, Publishing Director
Jukka Heiskanen, Editor-in-Chief, Comics
Juha Mäkinen, Editor, Comics
Jan Schulte-Tigges, Art Director, Comics
Henri Sarimo, Graphic Designer
Nathan Cosby, Freelance Editor

ROVIO

Thanks to Jukka Heiskanen, Juha Mäkinen, and the Kaiken team for their hard work and invaluable assistance.

ISBN: 978-1-63140-653-9

19 18 17 16 2 3 4 5

IDW®
www.IDWPUBLISHING.com

Ted Adams, CEO & Publisher
Greg Goldstein, President & COO
Robbie Robbins, EVP/Sr. Graphic Artist
Chris Ryall, Chief Creative Officer/Editor-in-Chief
Matthew Ruzicka, CPA, Chief Financial Officer
Dirk Wood, VP of Marketing
Lorelei Bunjes, VP of Digital Services
Jeff Webber, VP of Licensing, Digital and Subsidiary Rights
Jerry Bennington, VP of New Product Development

Facebook: **facebook.com/idwpublishing**
Twitter: **@idwpublishing**
YouTube: **youtube.com/idwpublishing**
Tumblr: **tumblr.idwpublishing.com**
Instagram: **instagram.com/idwpublishing**

ANGRY BIRDS COMICS, VOLUME 4: FLY OFF THE HANDLE. SEPTEMBER 2016. SECOND PRINTING. © 2009-2016 Rovio Entertainment Ltd. Rovio, Angry Birds, Bad Piggies, Mighty Eagle and all related titles, logos and characters are trademarks of Rovio Entertainment Ltd. All Rights Reserved. © 2016 Idea and Design Works, LLC. The IDW logo is registered in the U.S. Patent and Trademark Office. IDW Publishing, a division of Idea and Design Works, LLC. Editorial offices: 2765 Truxtun Road, San Diego, CA 92106. Any similarities to persons living or dead are purely coincidental. With the exception of artwork used for review purposes, none of the contents of this publication may be reprinted without the permission of Idea and Design Works, LLC. Printed in Korea.
IDW Publishing does not read or accept unsolicited submissions of ideas, stories, or artwork.

Originally published in ANGRY BIRDS COMICS, VOL. 2 issues #1–4.

WRITTEN BY: PAUL TOBIN • ART BY: PACO RODRIQUES • COLORS BY: DIGIKORE • LETTERS BY: PISARA OY

AHHH, HOW REFRESHING. IT'S ANOTHER BEAUTIFUL MORNING.
A QUICK SHOWER, AND THEN IT'S TIME TO START THE DAY.
I WONDER WHERE THE OTHER BIRDS ARE.
BOUND
BOUND
BOUND
CHUCK?
MATILDA?
BOMB?
HMMM. USUALLY I CAN AT LEAST HEAR THE BOYS PLAYING.
OR DESTROYING SOMETHING.

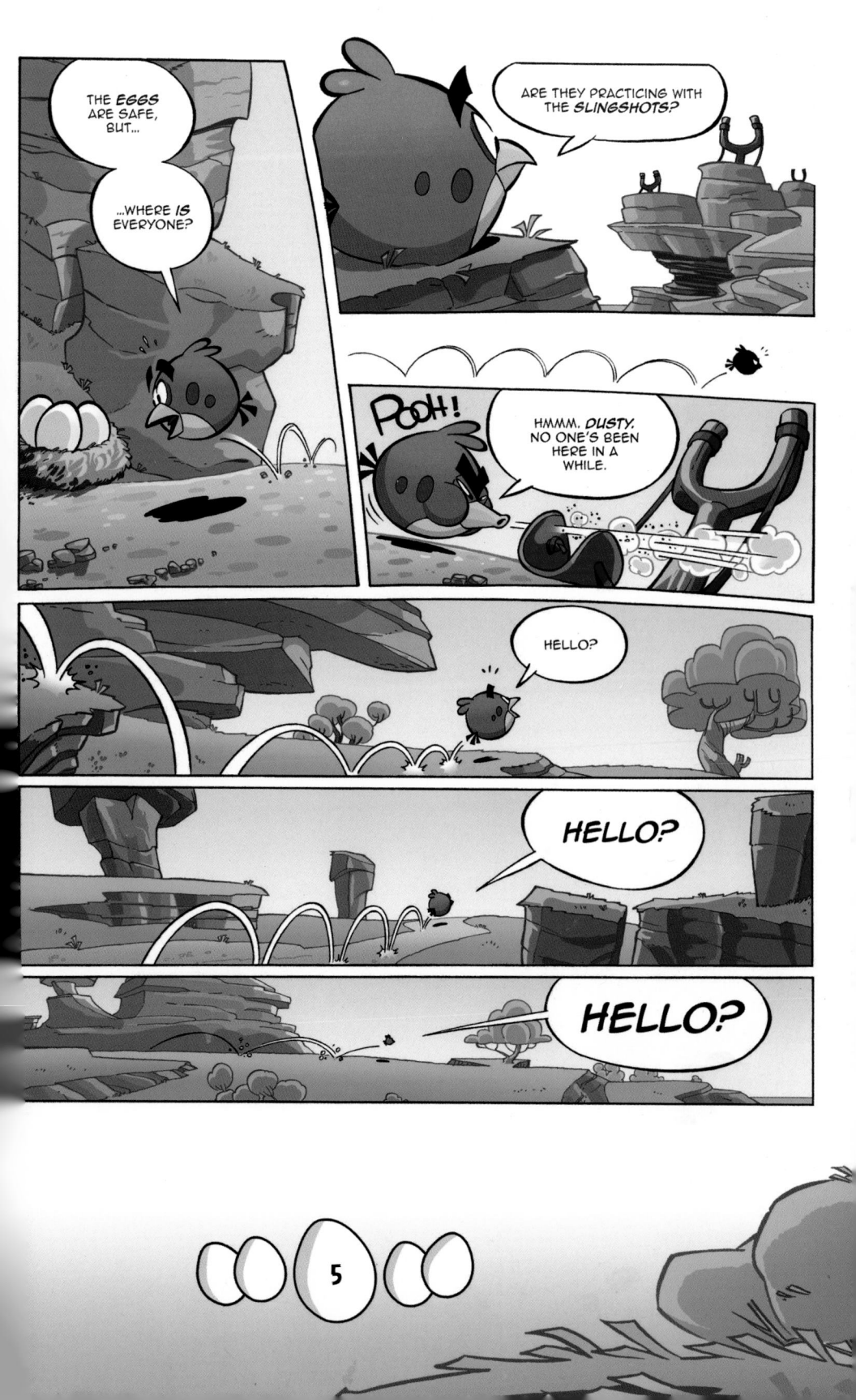
THE EGGS ARE SAFE, BUT...
...WHERE IS EVERYONE?
ARE THEY PRACTICING WITH THE SLINGSHOTS?
Pooh!
HMMM. DUSTY. NO ONE'S BEEN HERE IN A WHILE.
HELLO?
HELLO?
HELLO?

SOUTH BEACH...
HELLO?
SQUARE FOREST...
HELLO?
THE COBALT PLATEAUS...
HELLO?
THE CROWN MOUNTAINS
ANYBODY?
THE BAMBOO FOREST.
HELLO? HELLO?
WHERE IS EVERY-ONE?!!!

I'M... ALONE?
COULD THEY HAVE FALLEN DOWN A HOLE?
BEEN SWEPT OUT TO SEA?
CAUGHT IN AN AVALANCHE?
OR... WAIT A SECOND...

THE PIGS!
SOON, AT THE GATES...
RUMBLE
RUMBLE
RUMBLE
RUMBLE
RUMBLE
RUMBLE
?
!
HALT!
OR... NOT.

WHERE ARE THEY?
WHAT HAVE YOU DONE WITH THEM?
THOOP!
THOOP!
SPLONNG!
GRRRRR.
WE DON'T HAVE THE EGGS!
I PROMISE!
I PROMISE TWICE!
I'M NOT TALKING ABOUT THE EGGS!
NO EGGS! I PROMISE THAT I PROMISE!
WHERE ARE THE BIRDS?
WHERE ARE MY FRIENDS?
THWAKK!
WHAKK!
SMAKK!
RE THEY IN HERE?!!
CRASSSHH
KEE-RASSSHHHH!
???
YAHHH!

WHERE ARE THEY?
THEY'RE NOT HERE!
GRRRR! ONE LAST TIME... WHERE ARE THEY?!!
WE REALLY DON'T KNOW!
TO BE HONEST, THERE ARE A LOT OF THINGS WE DON'T KNOW!
WE'RE REALLY GOOD AT NOT KNOWING THINGS.
WE ARE!
HMMM.
YOU THINK THERE'S ANYBODY BETTER AT NOT KNOWING THINGS?
HMM, TO BE HONEST, I DON'T KNOW.
BUT THEN... WHERE ARE THEY?
CAN IT BE THAT MY FRIENDS ARE JUST... GONE?

AM I... ALONE?
SNIFF
SHUFFLE!
?
HUH?
SHUFFLE!

SURPRISE!
AHHHHH!
HAPPY BIRTHDAY, RED!
CHUCK! BOMB! MATILDA! JAY! JIM! JAKE! TERENCE! WHERE HAVE YOU ALL BEEN?
WE'VE BEEN IN HIDING!
PLANNING YOUR SURPRISE PARTY!
WHY? DID YOU GET LONELY?
HUH?
ME?
LONELY?
NEVER.
SNIFF
THE END.

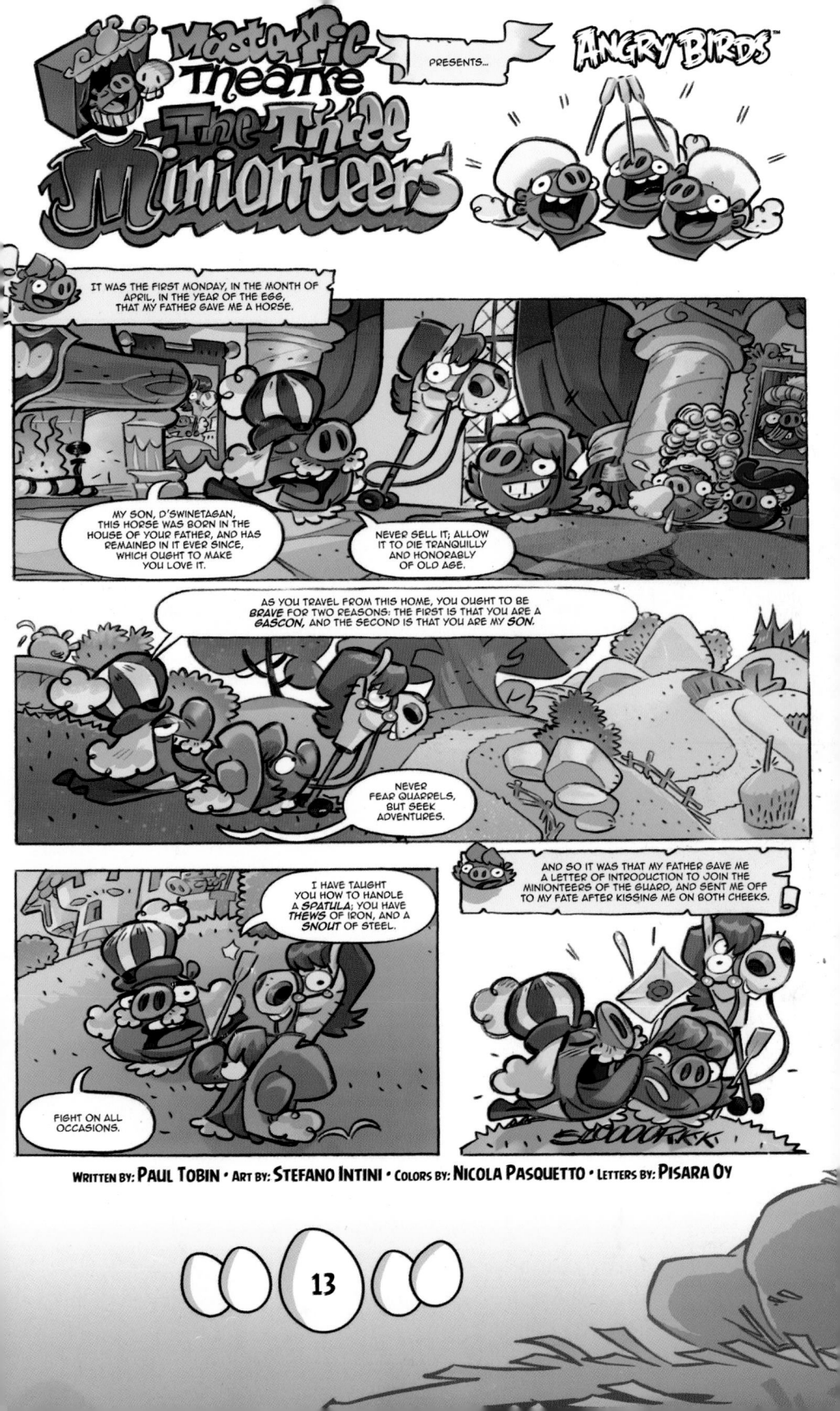

WRITTEN BY: PAUL TOBIN • ART BY: STEFANO INTINI • COLORS BY: NICOLA PASQUETTO • LETTERS BY: PISARA OY

I SET OFF FOR PARIS WITH A HEART YEARNING FOR ADVENTURE AND THE COMPANIONSHIP OF MY GOOD HORSE, CLYDE.
CLOP
CLOP
CLOP
PARIS
FIGHT SCENE
YOU CAN IMAGINE, THEN, THE RAGE INSTILLED IN MY HEART WHEN, STOPPING AT A LOCAL TROUGH, I OVERHEARD A POMPOUS AND IMPERTINENT PERSONAGE MAKING FUN OF MY NOBLE FAMILY STEED.
THIS HORSE IS A PIMPLE! A TOAD! I'VE SEEN NOSTRIL HAIRS WITH MORE NOBILITY.
HA HA
Café
THE BIRD HAD BLACK AND PIERCING EYES, A RED COMPLEXION, A STRONGLY MARKED BEAK, AND A BLACK AND WELL-SHAPED MUSTACHE. I DISLIKED HIM AT ONCE, AND EVEN AT TWICE.
AND SO WE FOUGHT! FLASHING SPATULAS! THE CHAOS OF BATTLE! THE VERY PULSE OF ADVENTURE!
I HAD NO CHOICE BUT TO CHALLENGE THIS MAN TO A DUEL.
I CHALLENGE YOU!
CHALLENGE HIM CHALLENGE HIM CHALLENGE HIM

THE BATTLE LASTED TWO SECONDS. I WAS SOUNDLY BEATEN. AND MY LETTER OF INTRODUCTION WAS STOLEN.
HA-HA HA-HA HA-HA HA
ADVENTURING IS HARD WORK, CLYDE.
AND SO IT WAS THAT I RODE INTO PARIS IN DISGRACE.
LOOK MOMMY, A DISGRACE!
WITHOUT MY LETTER OF INTRODUCTION, I WAS REFUSED ENTRY INTO THE MINIONTEERS.
I REFUSE!
AND IT WAS THEN THAT I SAW, FROM A WINDOW, THE VERY BIRD WHO HAD BESTED ME IN COMBAT! A BIRD KNOWN AS...

CARDINAL CARDINALIEU!
WAIT! I WANT TO MAKE COMBAT WITH YOU AGAIN, YOU FOUL FOWL!
BUT AS CHANCE WOULD HAVE IT, IN MY HASTE TO JOIN BATTLE, I MANAGED TO OFFEND THREE OTHERS.
BUMP
FIRST WAS HAMTHOS.
SWINE! I CHALLENGE YOU!
ACCEPTED!
AND THEN PORKIS!
K-THUMP
SPLOSHH!
BUFFON! WE MUST DUEL!
BE WITH YOU IN A SECOND!
AND FINALLY ARAMPIGS.
TUMBLE
BY MY SPATULA, WE DUEL!
TAKE A NUMBER!
CRASH

IT WAS THEN THAT A REALIZATION STRUCK ME. I HAD JUST CHALLENGED THREE DIFFERENT MINIONTEERS! COULD I DEFEAT THEM?
OOPSIES!
IT SEEMED UNLIKELY, FOR THEY WERE RUGGED INDIVIDUALS, AS NOBLE AS THE DAY IS LONG AND WELL-VERSED IN THE ART OF SPATULA-FIGHTING. STILL, AS A GASCON, I COULD ONLY DO AS MY FATHER HAD BADE ME.
WOOO WOOO! LET'S FIGHT!
DUELING, SIRS, IS ILLEGAL.
WHO DARES INTERRUPT?
A LOT OF US.
IT WAS CARDINAL CARDINALIEU'S GUARDS. EVIL MEN, ALL. THAT SAID, CREDIT MUST BE GIVEN WHERE CREDIT IS DUE, AND THE GUARD HAD CERTAINLY SPOKEN TRUTH: THERE WERE INDEED A LOT OF THEM.

MORE'S THE BETTER FOR THE FIGHT!
EN GARDE, SIR!
EN GARDE, EVERYONE!
WHEN THE BATTLE HAD ENDED, I AND THE THREE MINIONTEERS HAD DEFEATED A FORCE THAT WAS NEARLY FIVE TIMES OUR NUMBER, AND AT LEAST SEVEN TIMES AS BEAKY.
MY OWN PART IN THE BATTLE WAS RECOGNIZED BY KING CHEWY THE THIRTEENTH, AND IN RECOGNITION OF MY GALLANTRY AND BATTLE PROWESS, I WAS AWARDED A PLACE IN THE GUARD AND FORTY GOLD COINS. (WHICH WAS TOTALLY COOL!)
KING CHEWY

IT WAS SHORTLY THEREAFTER THAT I FELL IN LOVE WITH A YOUNG WOMAN NAMED CONSTANCE. (ALSO TOTALLY COOL!)
MY BELOVED CONSTANCE WORKED WITH ANNE, THE QUEEN CONSORT OF FRANCE, A WOMAN WHO WAS HAVING A SECRET AFFAIR WITH THE DUKE OF BUCKINGHAM-N-EGGS.
HEY! ARE YOU TWO KISSING?
SHHHH! IT'S SECRET!
CONSTANCE BEGGED ME TO RETRIEVE JEWELS THAT ANNE HAD GIVEN TO THE DUKE, AS ANNE NEEDED TO WEAR THEM AT THE ROYAL HOG STOMP. IF THEY WERE NOT AROUND HER DELICATE NECK AT THE TIME OF THE DANCE, HER AFFAIR WOULD BE REVEALED!
I COULD NOT REFUSE MY LOVE CONSTANCE THIS REQUEST, FOR I WAS SO MUCH IN LOVE WITH HER THAT I COULD REFUSE HER NOTHING. NOTHING AT ALL!
QUITE UNFORTUNATELY, CARDINAL CARDINALIEU AND HIS EVIL GUARDS STOOD IN MY WAY!
COULD I HAVE THAT LAST SLICE OF PIZZA?
HUH? OH! UMM. UHH.... ERRRR...
EXCUSE ME, BUT COULD YOU STAND SOMEWHERE ELSE?

I COULD NOT *HOPE* TO WIN PAST THE BIRDS *ALONE*, BUT AS FATE WOULD HAVE IT, MY THREE NOBLE FRIENDS CAME TO THE RESCUE. *HAMTHOS! PORKIS!* AND *ARAMPIGS!*

ALL FOR *ONE*, AND *ONE* FOR *ALL!*

NOW, *HOW* SHALL WE *HANDLE* THIS?

YOU KNOW, PROPER *DISCOURSE* COULD LEAD TO AN *EQUITABLE AGREEMENT*. LET'S *TALK* TO THEM AND TRY TO WORK OUT A *REASONABLE* SOLUTION.

HA HA HA HA HA HA HA HA HAW HAW HA HAW HAW HA HAW"

WE FIGHT!

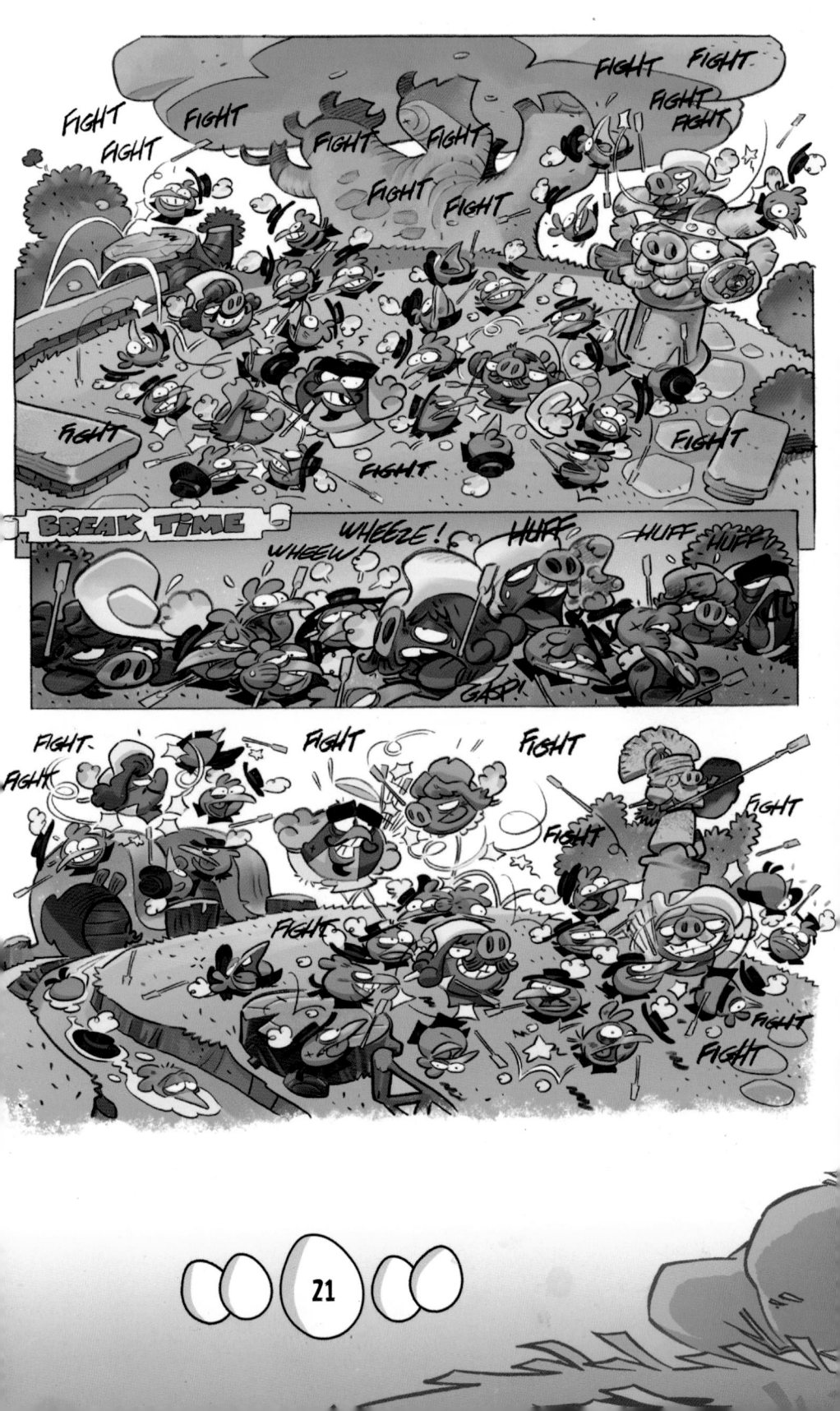
FIGHT
FIGHT
FIGHT
FIGHT
FIGHT
FIGHT
FIGHT
FIGHT
FIGHT
FIGHT
FIGHT
FIGHT
FIGHT
FIGHT
BREAK TIME
WHEEZE!
HUFF
HUFF
HUFF
WHEEW!
GASP!
FIGHT
FIGHT
FIGHT
FIGHT
FIGHT
FIGHT
FIGHT
FIGHT

VICTORY!
AND HERE'S THOSE JEWELS WE WERE LOOKING FOR!
ROYAL JEWELS! ALL FOR $1, AND $1 FOR ALL!
YOU GUYS ARE TOTALLY HEROES!
SMEK
WE KNOW!
HA HA HA
MUNCH
HAH! LET'S EAT PIZZA!
MUNCH
HA HA
ANYBODY MIND IF I EAT THE LAST ONE?
WE FIGHT!
The end

WRITTEN BY: PASCAL OOST • ART AND COLORS BY: THOMAS CABELLIC • LETTERS BY: ROVIO COMICS

WRITTEN BY: KARI KORHONEN • ART BY: CÉSAR FERIOLI • COLORS BY: DIGIKORE • LETTERS BY: PISARA OY

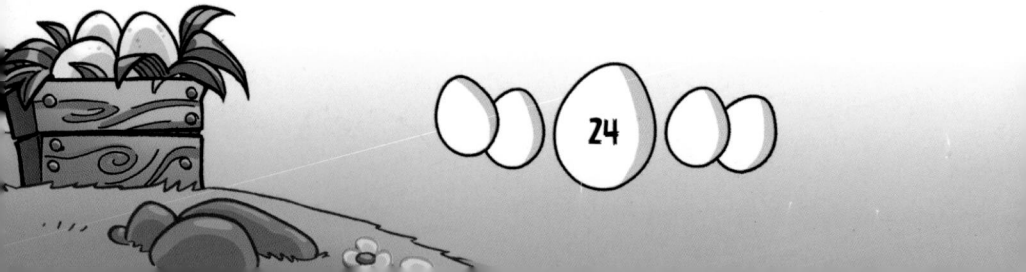

"TO THE RIGHT OF YOU!" HEH! HEH!
THAT'S PRETTY FUNNY!
AH! HAH! HAH! HAH! HOW STUPID CAN YOU GET!
HAH! HAH! PANTS! HAH! HAH! HAH! NYAH! AAH!
WHOOSH!
THUD!
?!
CAREFUL, FELLAS! THAT'S THE ONE THEY CALL "DA BOMB!"
WHY DIDN'T HE EXPLODE?
TEE! HEE! HEE! HEE! HEE!

MUAH! HAH! HAH! HAH! HAH! HAH!
"FACES LIKE MOTOR-MASCOTS!"
WELL THAT WAS CERTAINLY NEW.
÷SNORT!÷ NYAH! HAH! HAH!
WHAT THE DEVIL WAS THAT?! NO BLAST?
I NEED TO GO AGAIN!
I CANNOT EXPLODE UNLESS I GET ANGRY! THINKING OF THAT JOKE TOOK ALL THE FIGHT OUT OF ME!
BUT THIS TIME I'LL CONCENTRATE!
I WON'T... GIGGLE!... THINK ABOUT... THEIR SNOUTS!
WHUM!

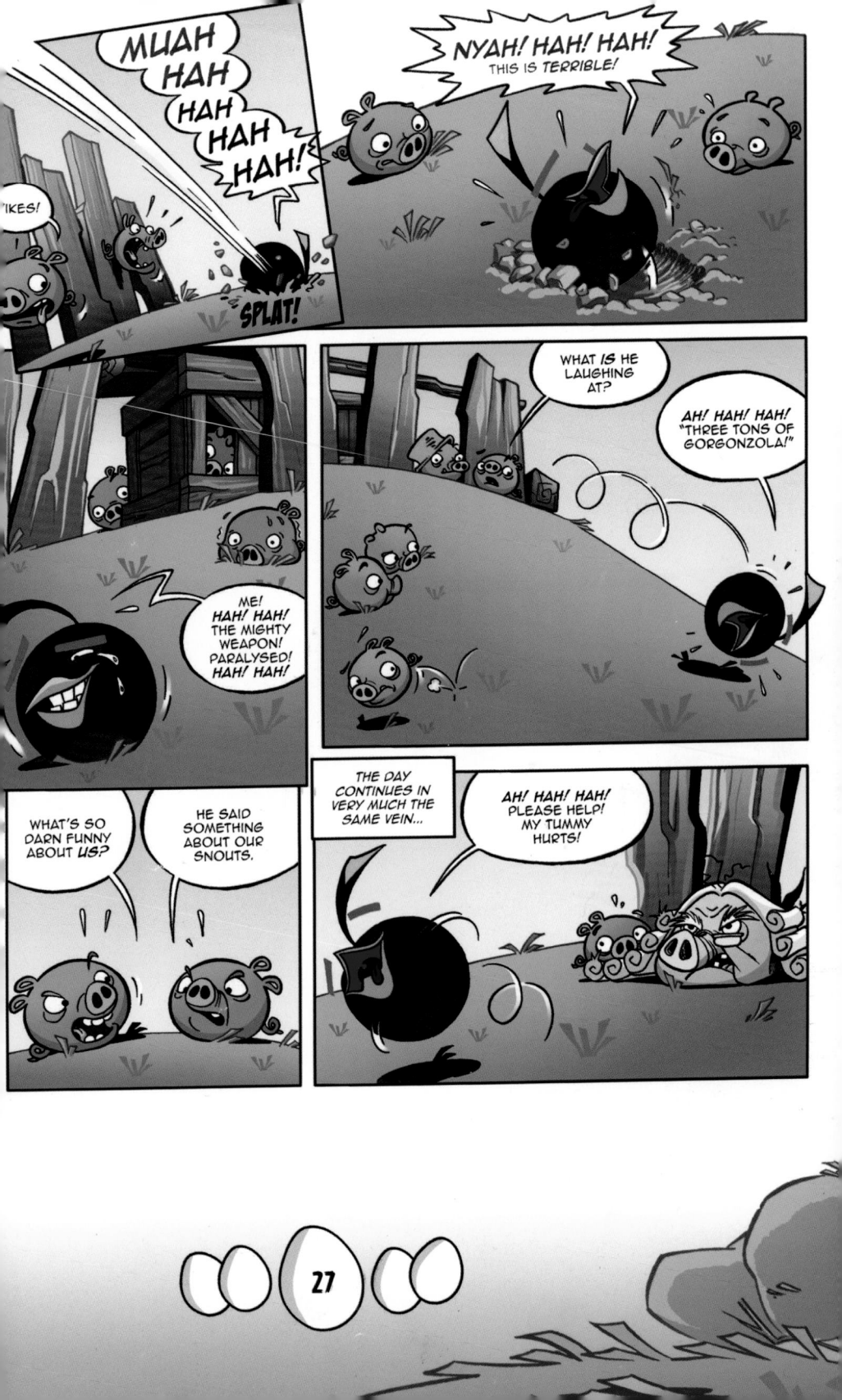
MUAH HAH HAH HAH HAH!
'IKES!
SPLAT!
NYAH! HAH! HAH! THIS IS TERRIBLE!
ME! HAH! HAH! THE MIGHTY WEAPON! PARALYSED! HAH! HAH!
WHAT IS HE LAUGHING AT?
AH! HAH! HAH! "THREE TONS OF GORGONZOLA!"
WHAT'S SO DARN FUNNY ABOUT US?
HE SAID SOMETHING ABOUT OUR SNOUTS.
THE DAY CONTINUES IN VERY MUCH THE SAME VEIN...
AH! HAH! HAH! PLEASE HELP! MY TUMMY HURTS!

YOU, SIR, ARE HIDEOUS! SNORT! YAH! HAH! HAH!

IT GETS SO BAD THAT THE MERE SITE OF PIGS GETS BOMB GOING!

WAAAAH HAH HAH!

IF THIS KEEPS UP, WE'LL BE IN REAL TROUBLE! WHAT'S WRONG WITH HIM?

BEATS ME!

NYAH HAH HAH HAH HAH!

SPLAT!

IF IT ISN'T... HAH! HAH! ...THE PORCINE PRINCE! NYAH! AH!

THE BIG PIG! WEE! HEE! HEE! PREPOSTEROUS!

"YOUR FACE!" AH! HAH! HAH!

GUARDS!

WHAT? IS HE LAUGHING AT *ME?* IS THAT IT?
TEE HEE
HEE HEE
HEE
WHAT'S WRONG WITH ME? GIVE IT TO ME HONESTLY! WHAT'S SO FREAKING FUNNY?
WELL, YOU DO HAVE A GIANT SNOZZLE.
DONK!
YOU'RE ONE TO TALK! LOOK IN THE MIRROR LATELY?
OR DID THE MIRROR CRACK?
THIS RIDICULE IS *UNLAWFUL!* I DEMAND AN ENQUIRY!
DARN!
HAH! HAH! HAH! HAH! HAH!

HIS HOOTING IS TEARING US APART! SOON THERE'LL BE NOTHING TO LAUGH ABOUT!
THERE'S NOTHING HERE TO LAUGH ABOUT!
BUT IF A GIGGLING MORON IS WHAT YOU ARE NOW... I SUPPOSE WE'LL DO ALL THE WORK!
WHAT?!
YOU ARE SUPPOSED TO GO BOOM! IT IS THE ONE THING ASKED OF YOU!
I MAY BE A MORON...
...BUT I DO MY PART!
BOOM!

I GUESS YOU'VE STILL GOT IT!
THERE! WAS THAT SO HARD?
ARE YOU JUDGING ME TOO?
KA-BOOM!
SOON...
THE PIGS STOPPED THEIR ATTACK! LET'S SEE WHAT'S GOING ON!
SO, THE ROYAL FACE IS SOMETHING TO LAUGH ABOUT NOW, IS IT?

THE PIGS HAVE BECOME A SOURCE OF AMUSEMENT, EH? WE'LL SEE ABOUT THAT!
HOW'S THAT FOR A JOKE!
SOON BACK IN THE FORTRESS...
YOU WILL NOT HAVE THE LAST LAUGH! LET US GO!
TELL ME WHAT THE ROUND BLACK ONE WAS HOWLING ABOUT!
IF YOU DON'T, WE'VE GOT WAYS TO MAKE LITTLE BIRDIES SING!
ELSEWHERE...
ALARM! THEY'VE GOT JAKE, JAY AND JIM!

YOU DO NOT DO THAT TO MY FRIENDS!
I WILL WIPE THAT GRIN OFF THEIR STUPID FACES OR MY NAME ISN'T...
STRETCH!
...DA BOMB!
AND SO...
YOU BOYS HAVE LEARNED YOUR LESSON, RIGHT?
THERE'S A TIME AND A PLACE FOR JOKES - EVEN GOOD ONES!
LET'S HEAR IT, THEN!
THERE WERE TWO PIGS...
I DON'T GET IT.
THE END

A MASTER PIG THEATER TALE

20,000 EGGS UNDER THE SEA

ANGRY BIRDS

WRITTEN BY: PAUL TOBIN • ART BY: PACO RODRIQUES • COLORS BY: JOSEP DE HARO • LETTERS BY: PISARA OY

WE SOON SET SAIL ON A SHIP ARMED WITH THE FINEST SLINGSHOTS THE NAVY COULD OFFER.

AND WE MOVED AT GOOD SPEED ACROSS THE WATERS.
FASTER! PUSH FASTER!
GRRRR! URRFF! HURGHH!

FOR SEVERAL DAYS, WE SCANNED THE HORIZONS, SEARCHING FOR THE DEADLY MONSTER.
HEY GUYS. WHAT ARE YOU DOING?
SCANNING THE HORIZON. SEARCHING FOR THE DEADLY MONSTER.

OH YEAH! THIS IS GOOD.
HAVING A LOT OF FUN, HERE. SCANNING THE HORIZON.
SEARRRRRRRRCHING FOR THE DEADLY MONSTER.

YEAH. THIS IS GREAT.

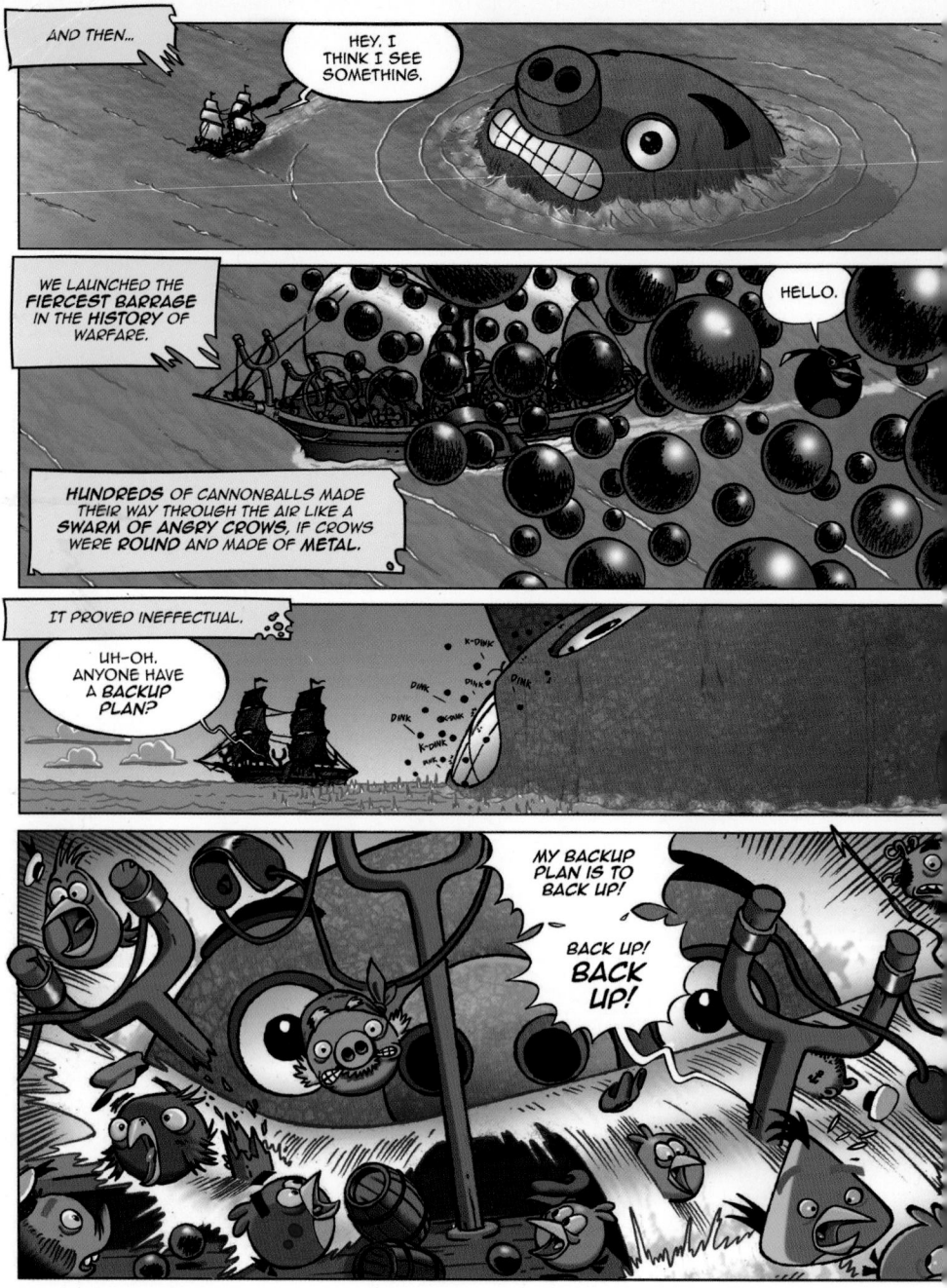
AND THEN...
HEY. I THINK I SEE SOMETHING.
WE LAUNCHED THE FIERCEST BARRAGE IN THE HISTORY OF WARFARE.
HELLO.
HUNDREDS OF CANNONBALLS MADE THEIR WAY THROUGH THE AIR LIKE A SWARM OF ANGRY CROWS, IF CROWS WERE ROUND AND MADE OF METAL.
IT PROVED INEFFECTUAL.
UH-OH. ANYONE HAVE A BACKUP PLAN?
K-DINK
DINK
DINK
DINK
DINK
K-DINK
K-DINK
MY BACKUP PLAN IS TO BACK UP!
BACK UP! BACK UP!

THE PRIMAL **ROAR** OF THE COLOSSAL BEAST WAS AS IF A **HURRICANE** HAD COME TO LIFE. OUR SHIP WAS ONLY AT **TOY** TO THIS CREATURE, AND THE TIMBERS SNAPPED LIKE THE **MEREST** OF TWIGS.

IN THE DESTRUCTION, MY MEN AND I WERE CAST ABOUT, WITH NO SENSE OF DIRECTION, OTHING **SOLID** WHERE WE COULD **STAND.** HERE WERE ONLY THE REAMS OF THE **BEAST,** AND A DESPERATE DESIRE TO **LIVE.**

MY PIZZA!

IN THE AFTERMATH, WITH OUR SHIP SUNK, WE CLUNG TO THE **ONLY POSSIBLE REMAINING SANCTUARY** TO KEEP US FROM **SINKING** TO THE **ENDLESS** DEPTHS BELOW...

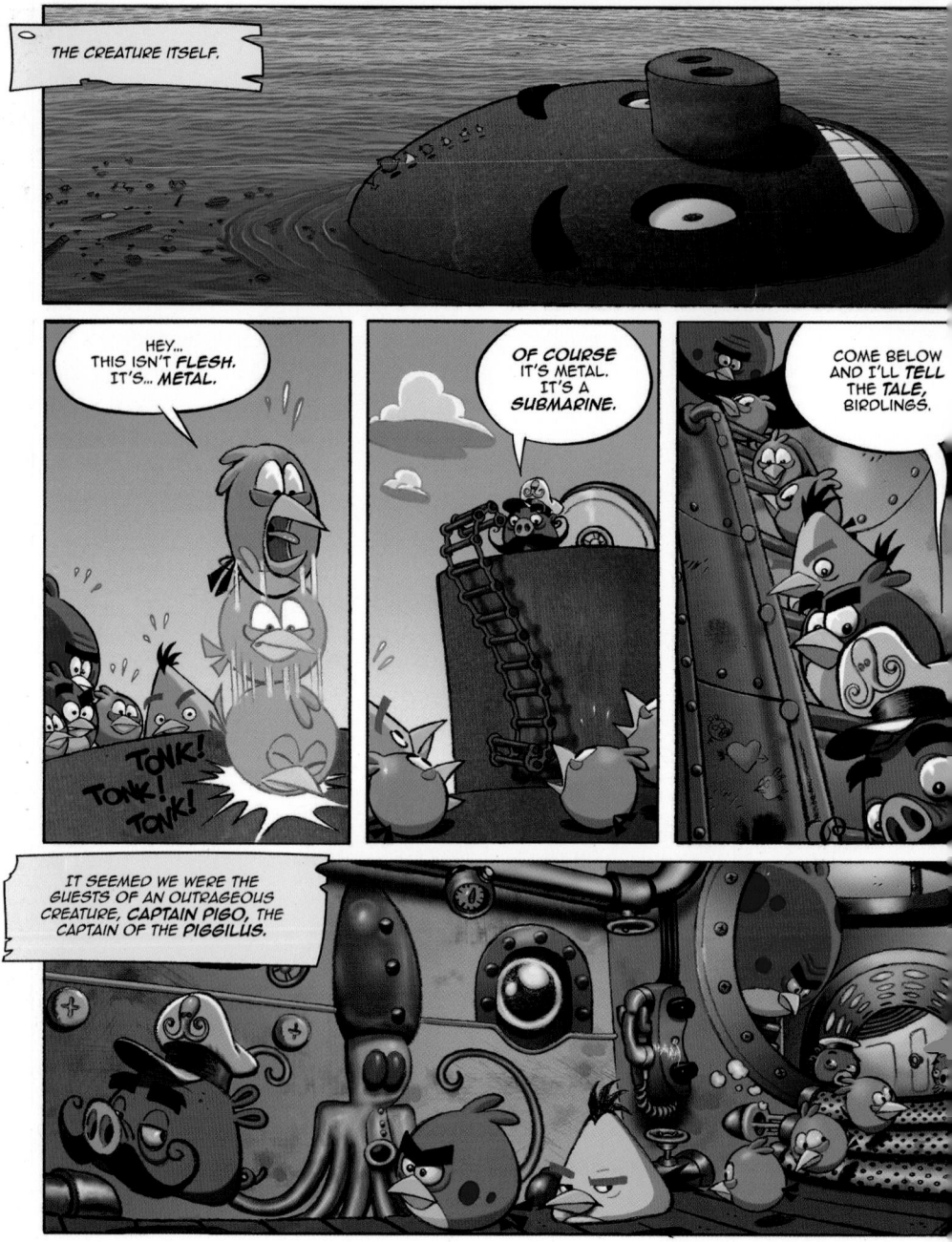
THE CREATURE ITSELF.
HEY... THIS ISN'T FLESH. IT'S... METAL.
TONK! TONK! TONK!
OF COURSE IT'S METAL. IT'S A SUBMARINE.
COME BELOW AND I'LL TELL THE TALE, BIRDLINGS.
IT SEEMED WE WERE THE GUESTS OF AN OUTRAGEOUS CREATURE, CAPTAIN PIGO, THE CAPTAIN OF THE PIGGILUS.

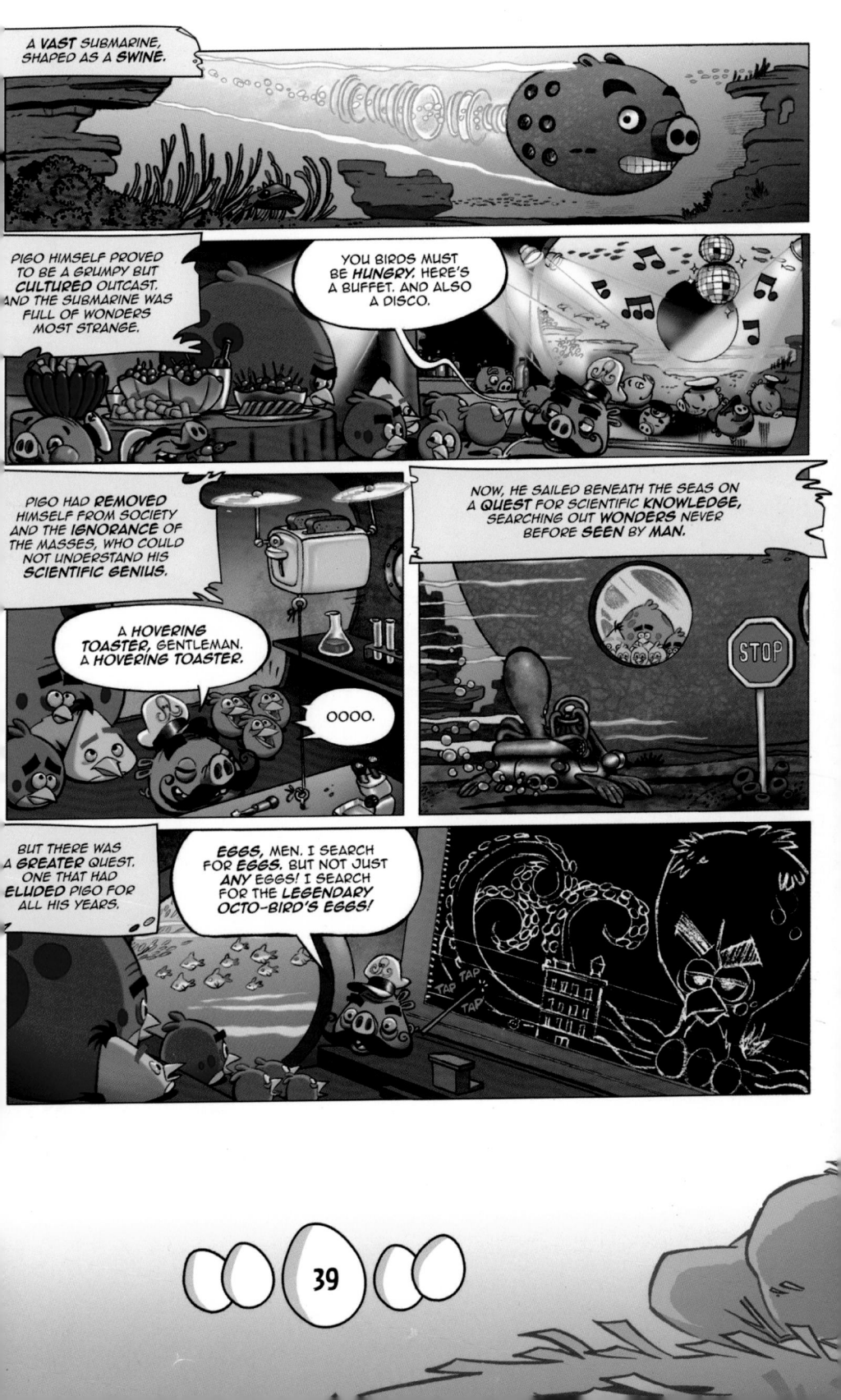
A VAST SUBMARINE, SHAPED AS A SWINE.
PIGO HIMSELF PROVED TO BE A GRUMPY BUT CULTURED OUTCAST. AND THE SUBMARINE WAS FULL OF WONDERS MOST STRANGE.
YOU BIRDS MUST BE HUNGRY. HERE'S A BUFFET. AND ALSO A DISCO.
PIGO HAD REMOVED HIMSELF FROM SOCIETY AND THE IGNORANCE OF THE MASSES, WHO COULD NOT UNDERSTAND HIS SCIENTIFIC GENIUS.
A HOVERING TOASTER, GENTLEMAN. A HOVERING TOASTER.
OOOO.
NOW, HE SAILED BENEATH THE SEAS ON A QUEST FOR SCIENTIFIC KNOWLEDGE, SEARCHING OUT WONDERS NEVER BEFORE SEEN BY MAN.
STOP
BUT THERE WAS A GREATER QUEST. ONE THAT HAD ELUDED PIGO FOR ALL HIS YEARS.
EGGS, MEN. I SEARCH FOR EGGS. BUT NOT JUST ANY EGGS! I SEARCH FOR THE LEGENDARY OCTO-BIRD'S EGGS!
TAP
TAP
TAP

DESPITE THE DESTRUCTION OF OUR SHIP, AND WHAT AMOUNTED TO OUR KIDNAPPING, WE BEGAN TO BE FRIENDS WITH THE RECLUSIVE CAPTAIN PIGO, SPENDING MANY DAYS IN QUIET REVERIE AND CONTEMPLATION.
HAH! TAKE THAT!
FINISH HIM!
AND WITNESSING THE STRANGEST OF WONDERS WHILE TWENTY THOUSAND LEAGUES BENEATH THE SEA.
I RECALL SUCH WONDERS AS THE ELECTRIC EEL, WHICH MADE THE OCEAN DEPTHS AS BRIGHT AS ANY LONDON STREET.
TURN THAT OFF! I'M TRYING TO SLEEP!
AND A THEME PARK WITH THE LARGEST WATER SLIDE I'D EVER SEEN.
19,998 LEAGUES
19,999 LEAGUES
20,000 LEAGUES
AND THEN CAME THE DAY WHEN THE ALARM BELLS RANG.
DING
DING
DING
SHOOP
SHOOP
SHOOP

HE OCTO-BIRD HAD BEEN SIGHTED.
MAN THE TORPEDOES!
HARD TO STARBOARD!
SEAL ALL HATCHES!
ALL STATIONS PREPARE FOR BATTLE, AND, MEN...
YES SIR?
RECORD MY FAVORITE CARTOONS. I DON'T WANT TO MISS THEM.
SECONDS LATER, THE BATTLE BEGAN. THE LASHING TENTACLES OF THE GREAT OCTO-BIRD STRUCK THE WALLS OF OUR SUBMARINE. THERE WAS A NOISE LIKE A HUNDRED THOUSAND BURSTS OF THUNDER.

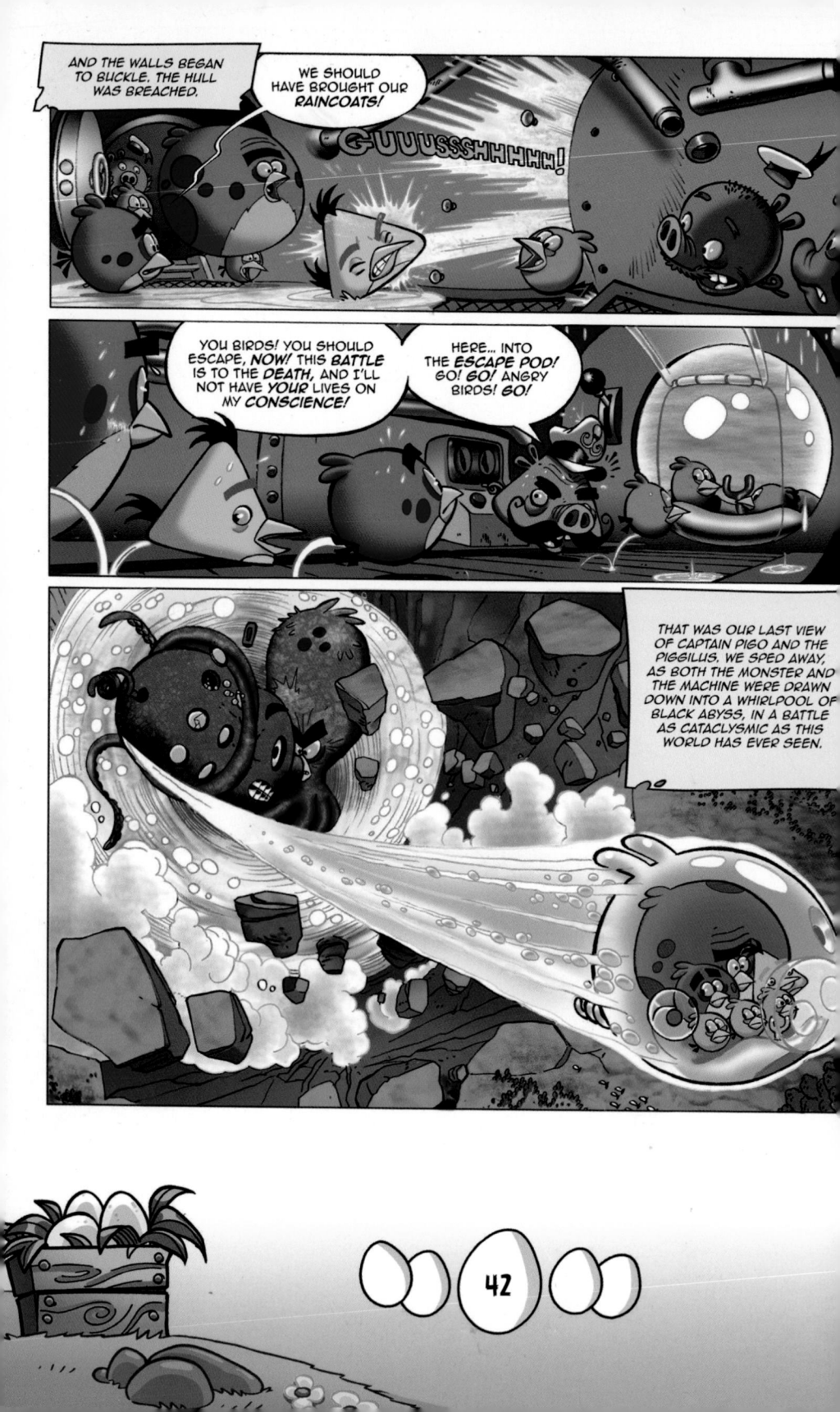
AND THE WALLS BEGAN TO BUCKLE. THE HULL WAS BREACHED.
WE SHOULD HAVE BROUGHT OUR RAINCOATS!
GUUUSSSHHHHH!
YOU BIRDS! YOU SHOULD ESCAPE, NOW! THIS BATTLE IS TO THE DEATH, AND I'LL NOT HAVE YOUR LIVES ON MY CONSCIENCE!
HERE... INTO THE ESCAPE POD! GO! GO! ANGRY BIRDS! GO!
THAT WAS OUR LAST VIEW OF CAPTAIN PIGO AND THE PIGGILUS. WE SPED AWAY, AS BOTH THE MONSTER AND THE MACHINE WERE DRAWN DOWN INTO A WHIRLPOOL OF BLACK ABYSS, IN A BATTLE AS CATACLYSMIC AS THIS WORLD HAS EVER SEEN.

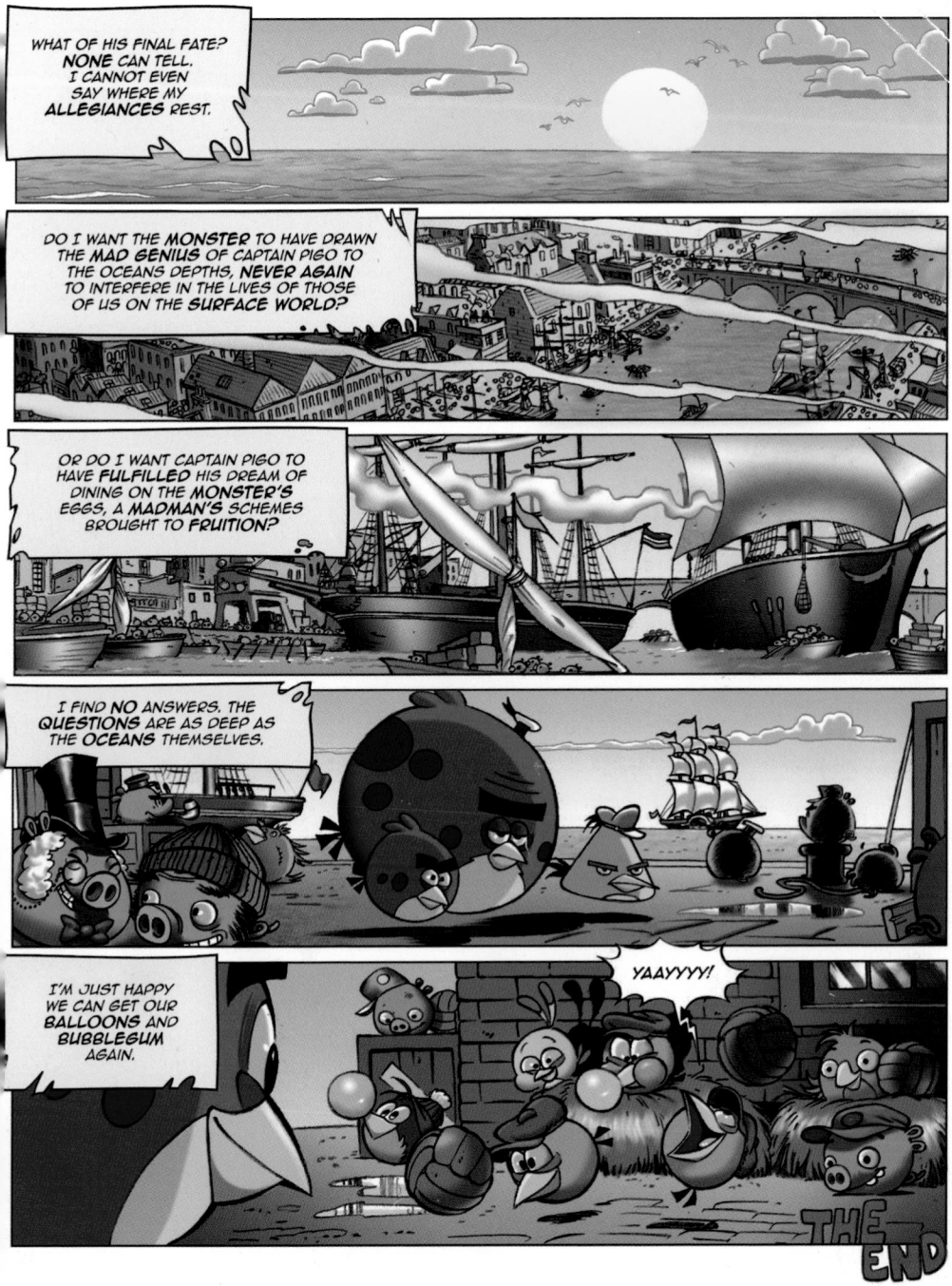
WHAT OF HIS FINAL FATE? NONE CAN TELL. I CANNOT EVEN SAY WHERE MY ALLEGIANCES REST.
DO I WANT THE MONSTER TO HAVE DRAWN THE MAD GENIUS OF CAPTAIN PIGO TO THE OCEANS DEPTHS, NEVER AGAIN TO INTERFERE IN THE LIVES OF THOSE OF US ON THE SURFACE WORLD?
OR DO I WANT CAPTAIN PIGO TO HAVE FULFILLED HIS DREAM OF DINING ON THE MONSTER'S EGGS, A MADMAN'S SCHEMES BROUGHT TO FRUITION?
I FIND NO ANSWERS. THE QUESTIONS ARE AS DEEP AS THE OCEANS THEMSELVES.
I'M JUST HAPPY WE CAN GET OUR BALLOONS AND BUBBLEGUM AGAIN.
YAAYYYY!
THE END

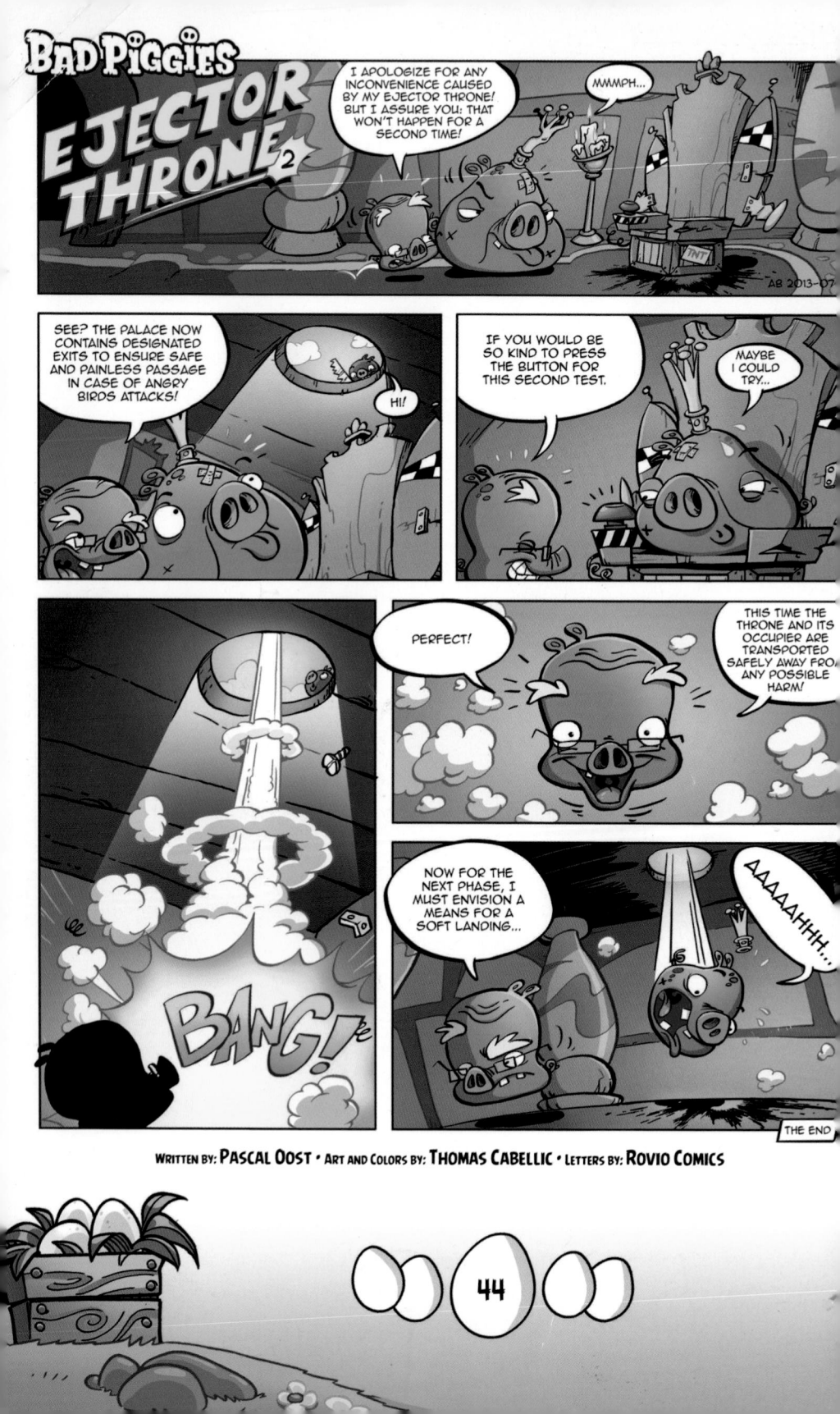

WRITTEN BY: PASCAL OOST • ART AND COLORS BY: THOMAS CABELLIC • LETTERS BY: ROVIO COMICS

WRITTEN BY: JANNE TORISEVA • ART BY: CÉSAR FERIOLI • COLORS BY: DIGIKORE • LETTERS BY: PISARA OY

HAT... CHOOO!
SNIRF! I'VE HAD ENOUGH OF THIS! SOMEONE BETTER DO SOMETHING!
SOON:
THE FLAMING ALLERGY NULLIFIER WILL SOLVE THE PROBLEM, YOUR MAJESTY.
IT'LL TURN THE FIRE INTO A STRONG WIND...
...WHICH WILL PUSH THE POLLEN AWAY.
FAN-TASTIC! MAKE HUNDREDS OF THOSE, IMMEDIATELY!
YOUR HIGHNESS! WITH ONE BIG MACHINE WE COULD STEAL THE EGGS FROM THE BIRDS!

HMM... THE WIND IS RISING.
YOU-HEAVE-HO!
?
WHAT ARE YOU LARDBALLS DOING HERE?
TURN THE GLASS!
YES, BOSS!
HEY! ~SNIFF~ TURN THAT THING OFF!
HATCHOOO!
GO GET THE EGGS!
YES, BOSS!

LOOK AT THOSE CLOUDS, GUYS!
LET'S GET BACK TO OUR MATES.
AYE.

WHAT'S WRONG WITH RED?
AND WHERE ARE THE EGGS?
AND *WHAT* IS THAT?
~SNEEZE~ THE PIGS
HATCHOO!

PIGS!
LET'S HOPE THAT THEY ARE NOT TOO FAR ALREADY!

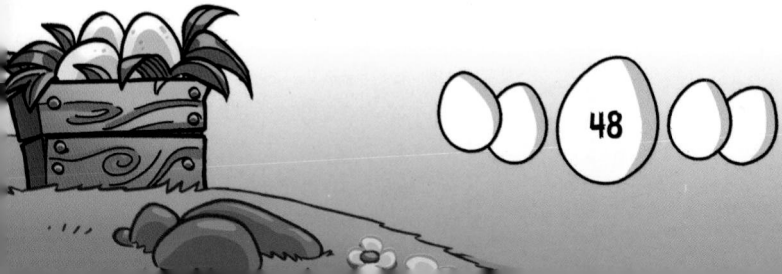

BLUE BIRDS APPROACHING!
PUSH FASTER, YOU LAZY PORK!
I'M DOING MY BEST!
CLOSE THE GATE!
WE DID IT!
THAT'S POINTLESS. THE GATE IS TOO STRONG.
THERE ARE MORE OF THOSE MACHINES. WHAT ARE THEY?
DUNNO, BUT I DON'T LIKE 'EM. THEY'RE TOO WINDY.
WINDY...? GUYS, WE MIGHT STILL HAVE A CHANCE!

MY DEAR EGGS! WELCOME HOME!
CHEF, WHAT ARE YOU WAITING FOR? MAKE ME AN OMELETTE!
WHAT'S THAT HUMMING SOUND BEHIND THE GATE...
IT WORKS!
OH NO, THE EGG-WAGON!
IT'LL CRASH INTO THE WALL!
HURRY, LET'S TURN THESE MACHINES OFF!
JUST IN TIME!

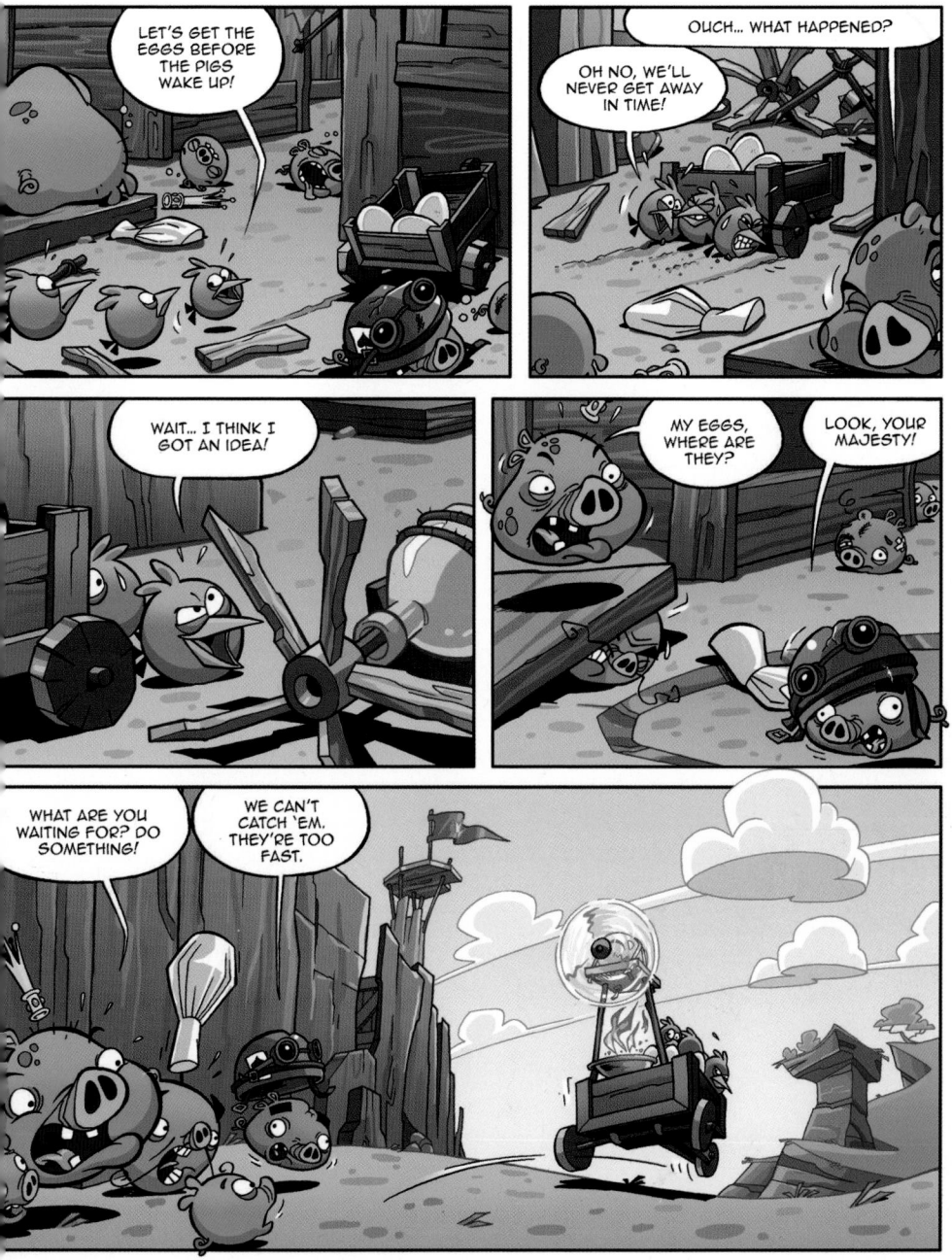
LET'S GET THE EGGS BEFORE THE PIGS WAKE UP!
OUCH... WHAT HAPPENED?
OH NO, WE'LL NEVER GET AWAY IN TIME!
WAIT... I THINK I GOT AN IDEA!
MY EGGS, WHERE ARE THEY?
LOOK, YOUR MAJESTY!
WHAT ARE YOU WAITING FOR? DO SOMETHING!
WE CAN'T CATCH 'EM. THEY'RE TOO FAST.

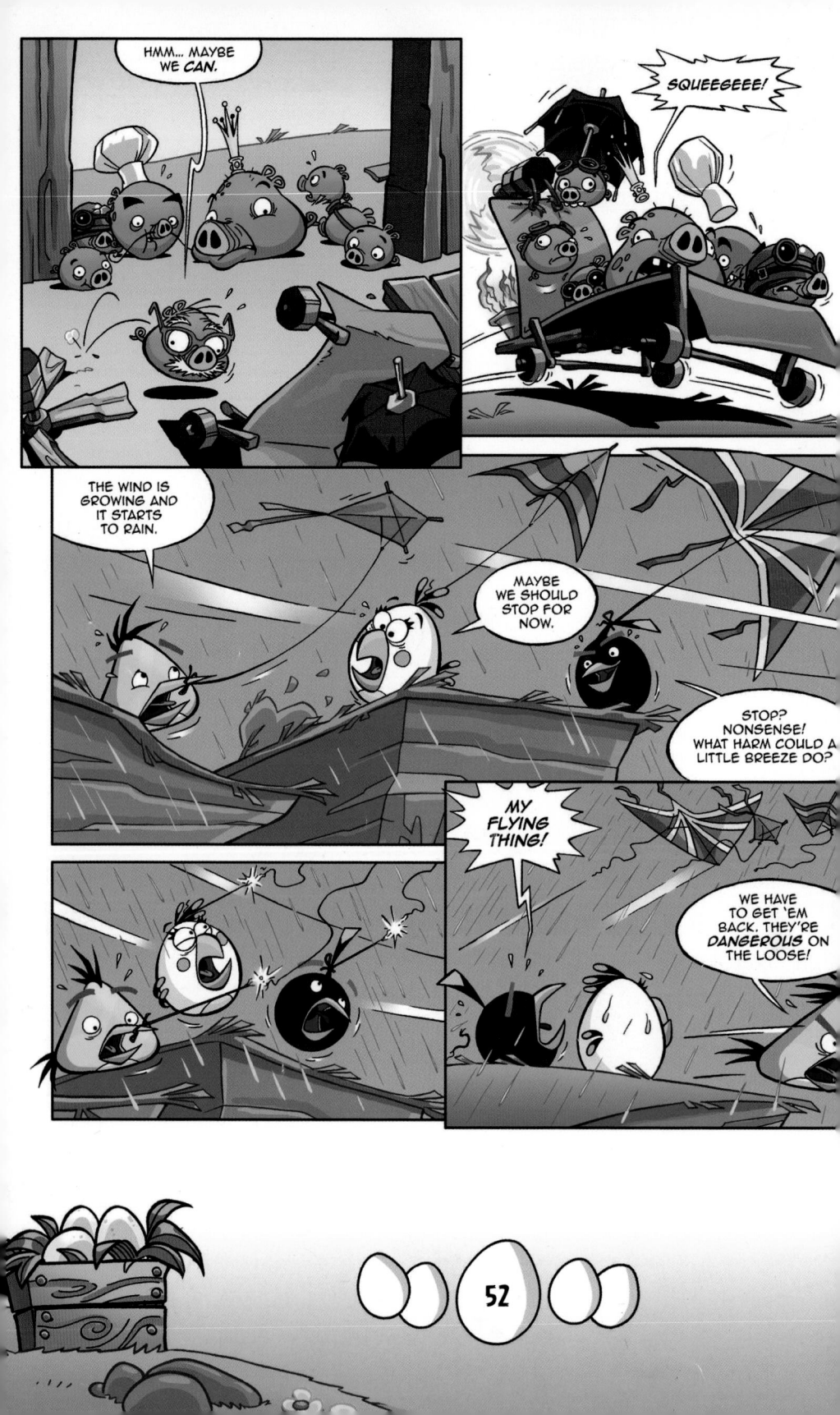
HMM... MAYBE WE CAN.
SQUEEGEEE!
THE WIND IS GROWING AND IT STARTS TO RAIN.
MAYBE WE SHOULD STOP FOR NOW.
STOP? NONSENSE! WHAT HARM COULD A LITTLE BREEZE DO?
MY FLYING THING!
WE HAVE TO GET 'EM BACK. THEY'RE DANGEROUS ON THE LOOSE!

THE PIGS ARE COPYING US! HOW RUDE!
DON'T WORRY, THEY CAN'T CATCH US. THEIR LOAD IS TOO HEAVY.
WHY ARE WE SLOWING DOWN?
OH NO, THE RAIN EXTINGUISHED THE FIRE!
CHEF, GET READY TO BOIL SOME EGGS!
YES, YOUR HIGHNESS!
HUH?
SQUEAL!

PHEW! THAT WAS AT THE LAST MOMENT!
BUT WHAT IN THE WORLD ARE THOSE?
PIGS!
EGGS!
MAYBE IT'S BETTER THIS WAY, BOMB.
BUT WHAT SHALL WE DO WITH THESE BACON BADDIES?
HMM... I SAY LET'S SEND THEM...
...WHERE THE WIND BLOWS!

WRITTEN BY: JANNE TORISEVA • ART BY: MARCO GERVASIO • COLORS BY: DIGIKORE • LETTERS BY: PISARA OY

AN HOUR LATER.
SEE, YOU JUST PREPARE THE GROUND BY HOEING AND RAKING.
RAKE RAKE RAKE
GRUMBLE GRUMBLE GRUMBLE
SCRATCH SCRATCH
A DAY LATER.
AND WE DROP THE SEEDS IN OUR ROWS.
GRUMBLE GRUMBLE GRUMBLE
A DAY LATER.
I HAVE THIS SPECIAL PLANT FOOD I MAKE FROM MUD FROM THE GEYSERS. IT'S VERY RICH IN NUTRIENTS.
HMMPF!
HMMPF!
HMMPF!
A WEEK LATER.
SEE? THE PLANTS GROW EXTRAORDINARILY FAST.
HEY, THIS IS KIND OF... FUN!
A WEEK AFTER THAT...
THIS IS AWESOME!
I LOVE GARDENING!
WE... WE DID IT!

WATERMELON, CUCUMBERS, RHUBARB, SUGAR CANE, POTATOES!
EVERYTHING'S GROWING!

AND HERE, TASTE THESE STRAWBERRIES FRESH FROM OUR GARDEN!
MUNCH
SLURP
WOW! THESE ARE DELICIOUS!
MUNCH

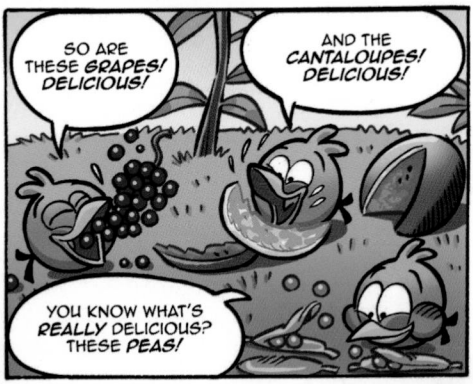
SO ARE THESE GRAPES! DELICIOUS!
AND THE CANTALOUPES! DELICIOUS!
YOU KNOW WHAT'S REALLY DELICIOUS? THESE PEAS!

DELICIOUS!
DELICIOUS!
SOOOOO DELICIOUS!
???

ARE THEY TALKING ABOUT EGGS?
NO. SOMETHING ELSE.
SHOULD WE, I MEAN, YOU THINK, MAYBE WE COULD... UMM...

IF YOU WERE GOING TO SUGGEST WE STEAL EVERYTHING, AND EAT IT, AND ALSO STEAL THE SEEDS AND MAKE OUR OWN GARDEN, AND EAT THAT, THEN...

YESSSSSS!!!

THE NEXT DAY...
WELL, THE THREE OF YOU ARE CERTAINLY UP EARLY.
YEP!
IT'S BECAUSE WE LOVE GARDENING!
WE DO! I WONDER IF ANYTHING NEW SPROUTED TODAY! MAYBE THERE'LL BE SOME...

UHHH.
GAHHH!
OH NO.

AHHHHHHHHHH!

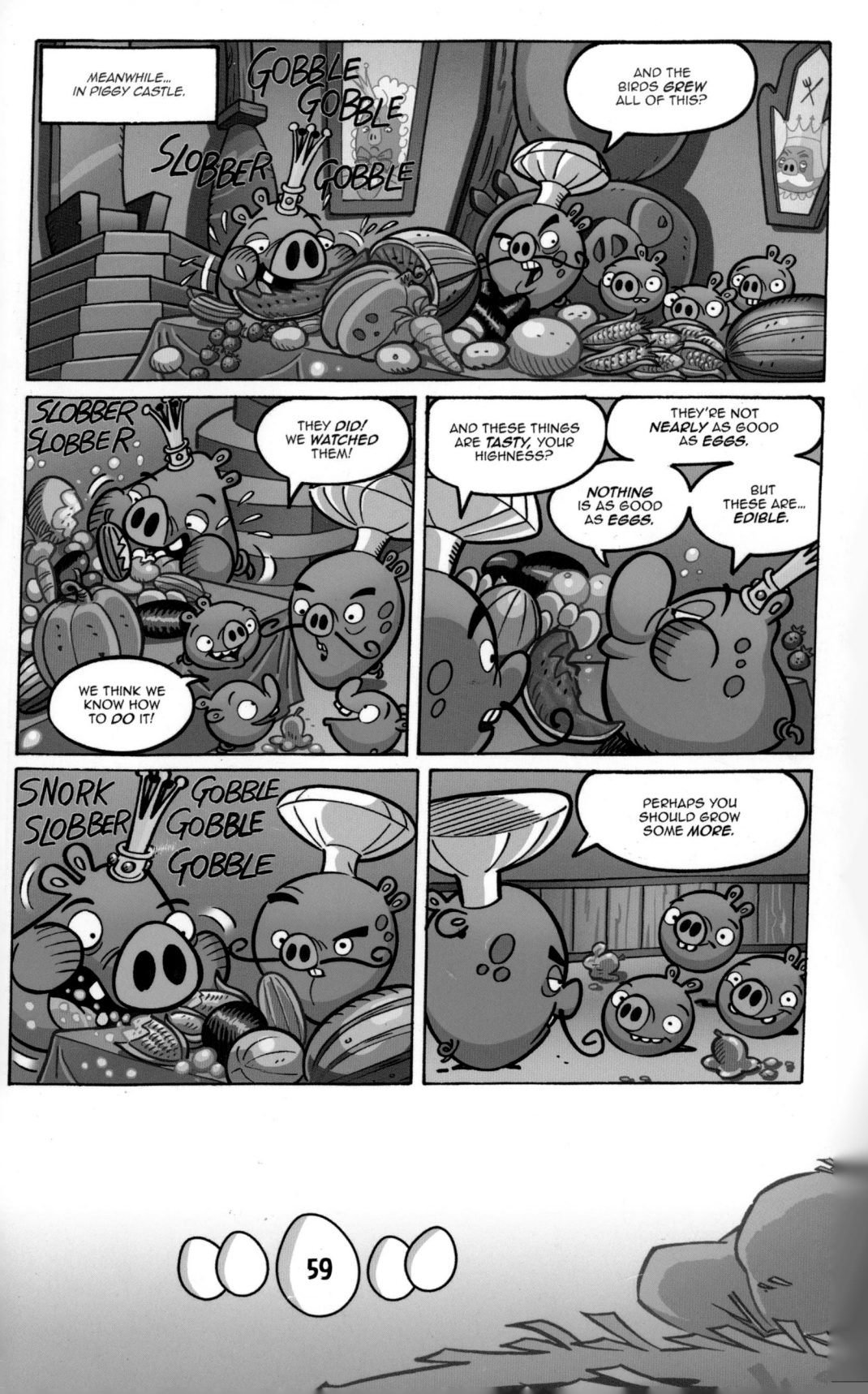
MEANWHILE... IN PIGGY CASTLE.
GOBBLE GOBBLE
SLOBBER GOBBLE
AND THE BIRDS GREW ALL OF THIS?
SLOBBER SLOBBER
THEY DID! WE WATCHED THEM!
WE THINK WE KNOW HOW TO DO IT!
AND THESE THINGS ARE TASTY, YOUR HIGHNESS?
THEY'RE NOT NEARLY AS GOOD AS EGGS.
NOTHING IS AS GOOD AS EGGS.
BUT THESE ARE... EDIBLE.
SNORK SLOBBER
GOBBLE GOBBLE GOBBLE
PERHAPS YOU SHOULD GROW SOME MORE.

AND SO...
THEY WERE USING RAKES AND HOES, LIKE THIS.
RAKE
RAKE
SCRATCH
SCRATCH
STAB
STAB

AND THEN THEY MADE *HOLES* IN THE *DIRT!*
AFTER *THAT,* THEY PUT *SEEDS* INSIDE THE *HOLES.*
SHOVEL
SHOVEL
SHOVEL

POUR THEM *ALL* IN.
SHAKE
SHAKE
SHAKE
YEAH! WHY WASTE TIME?
GOOD IDEA.

AND THEN THEY USED THIS *MUD* FROM THE GEYSERS. I GUESS IT MAKES THE PLANTS *GROW FASTER.*
HOW MUCH MUD DID THEY *USE?*
WHAT'S IT *MATTER?* USE IT *ALL.*

KERR-
FLOPP!!!

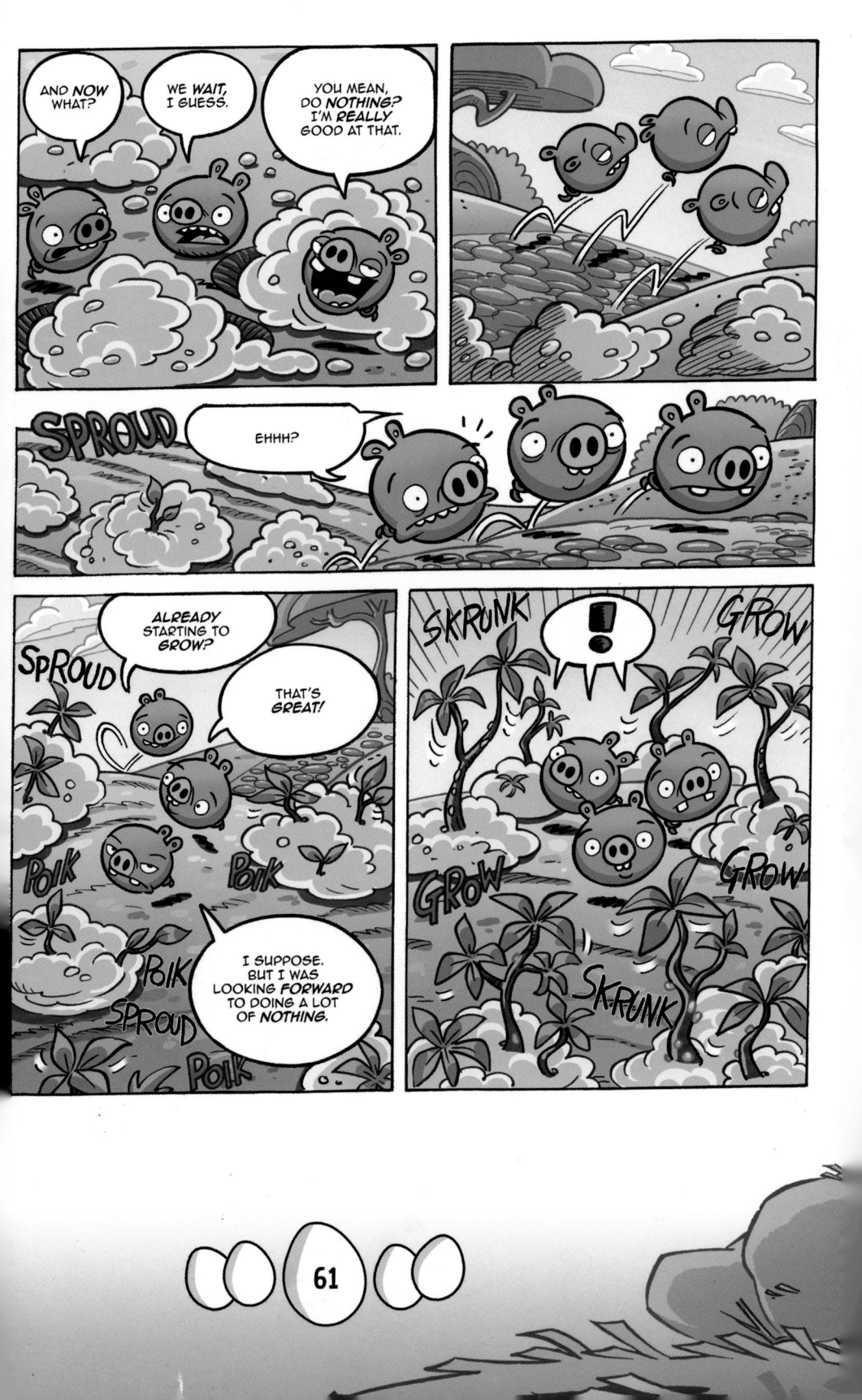
AND NOW WHAT?
WE WAIT, I GUESS.
YOU MEAN, DO NOTHING? I'M REALLY GOOD AT THAT.
SPROUD
EHHH?
SPROUD
ALREADY STARTING TO GROW?
THAT'S GREAT!
POIK
POIK
POIK
SPROUD
POIK
I SUPPOSE. BUT I WAS LOOKING FORWARD TO DOING A LOT OF NOTHING.
SKRUNK
!
GROW
GROW
GROW
SKRUNK

UHHHHHHH OH.

ARE THEY GOING TO STOP?
IT DOESN'T LOOK LIKE IT. MAYBE WE SHOULD DO SOMETHING?
AGAIN, I WAS LOOKING FORWARD TO DOING NOTHING.

OOOO! I'VE GOT AN IDEA OF WHAT WE COULD DO!
WHAT'S THAT?

RUNNNNNNN!!!

THE PLANTS ARE CATCHING US!!!
RUUUMBLE

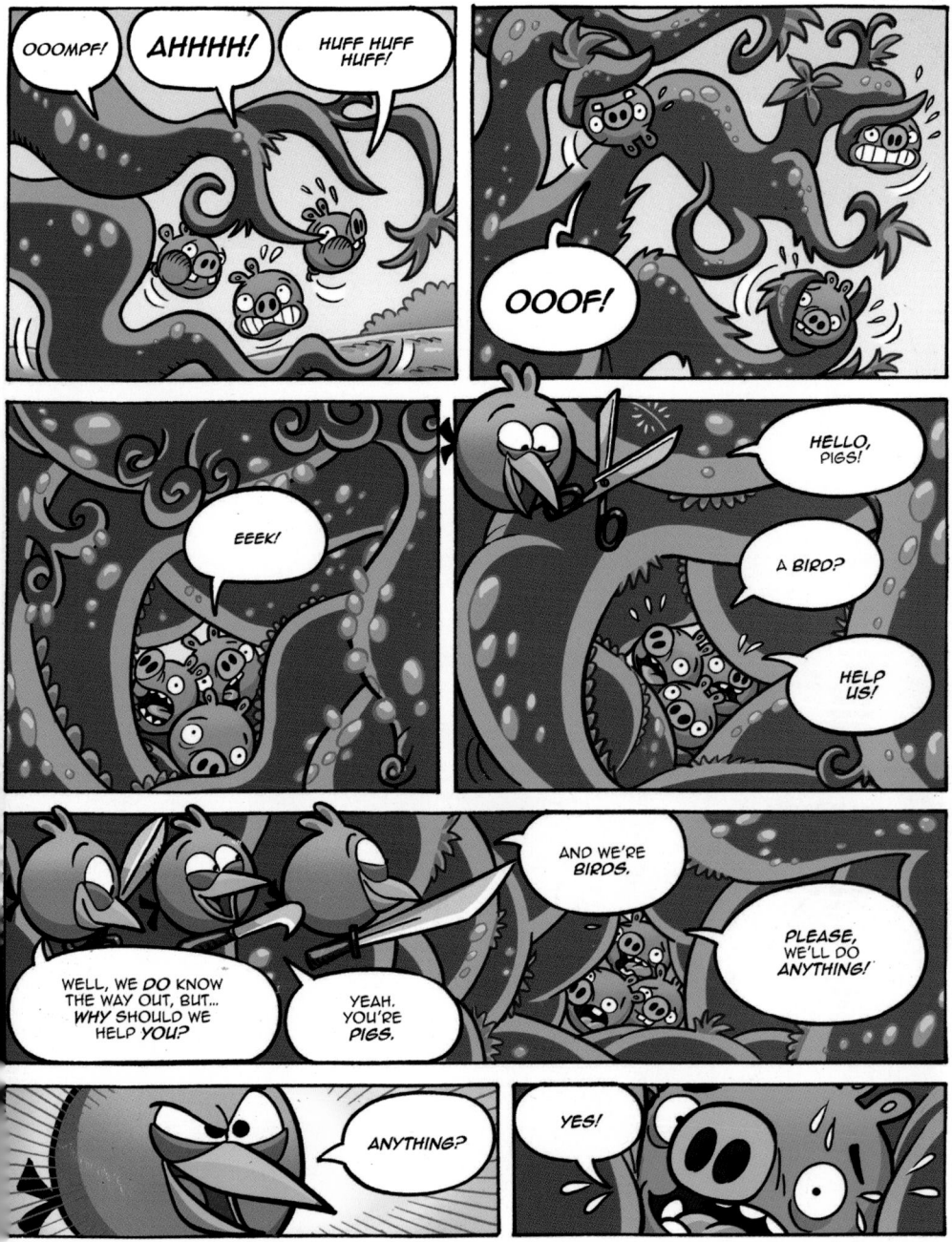
OOOMPF!
AHHHH!
HUFF HUFF HUFF!
OOOF!
EEEK!
HELLO, PIGS!
A BIRD?
HELP US!
AND WE'RE BIRDS.
PLEASE, WE'LL DO ANYTHING!
WELL, WE DO KNOW THE WAY OUT, BUT... WHY SHOULD WE HELP YOU?
YEAH. YOU'RE PIGS.
ANYTHING?
YES!

THE NEXT DAY.

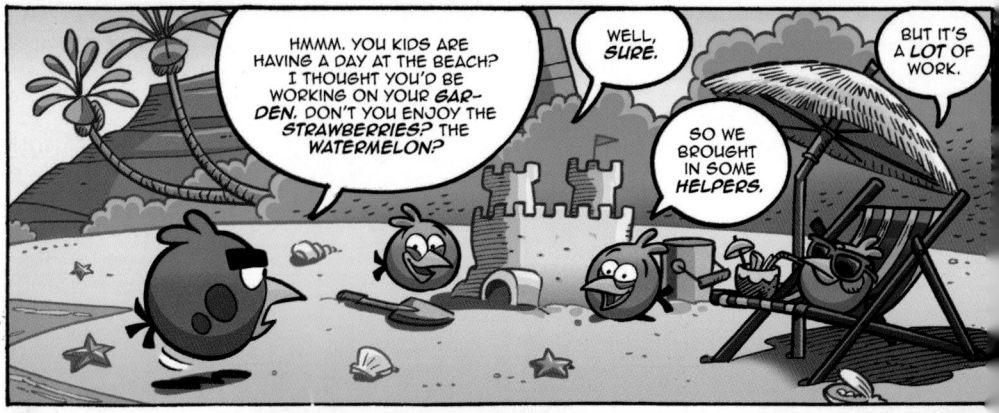
HMMM. YOU KIDS ARE HAVING A DAY AT THE BEACH? I THOUGHT YOU'D BE WORKING ON YOUR *SAR-DEN.* DON'T YOU ENJOY THE *STRAWBERRIES?* THE *WATERMELON?*
WELL, *SURE.*
BUT IT'S A *LOT* OF WORK.
SO WE BROUGHT IN SOME *HELPERS.*

HUFF HUFF HUFF!
GUHH! GAHHH!
THE END

WRITTEN BY: GLENN DAKIN • ART BY: CÉSAR FERIOLI • COLORS BY: DIGIKORE • LETTERS BY: PISARA OY

DAWN BREAKS OVER THE COBALT PLATEAU...
TO REVEAL...
YIKES! WHERE DID THAT COME FROM? WHA – WHAT IS IT?
IT – IT'S MAKING ME SHIVER AND SHAKE! BUT I DON'T KNOW WHY!
IT'S A SCARECROW! THE TRADITIONAL ENEMY OF THE BIRD RACE!
SUDDENLY...
LOOK OUT!
IT – IT'S MOVING!
BOMB'S EXPLODED WITH FRIGHT!
KA-BOOM!

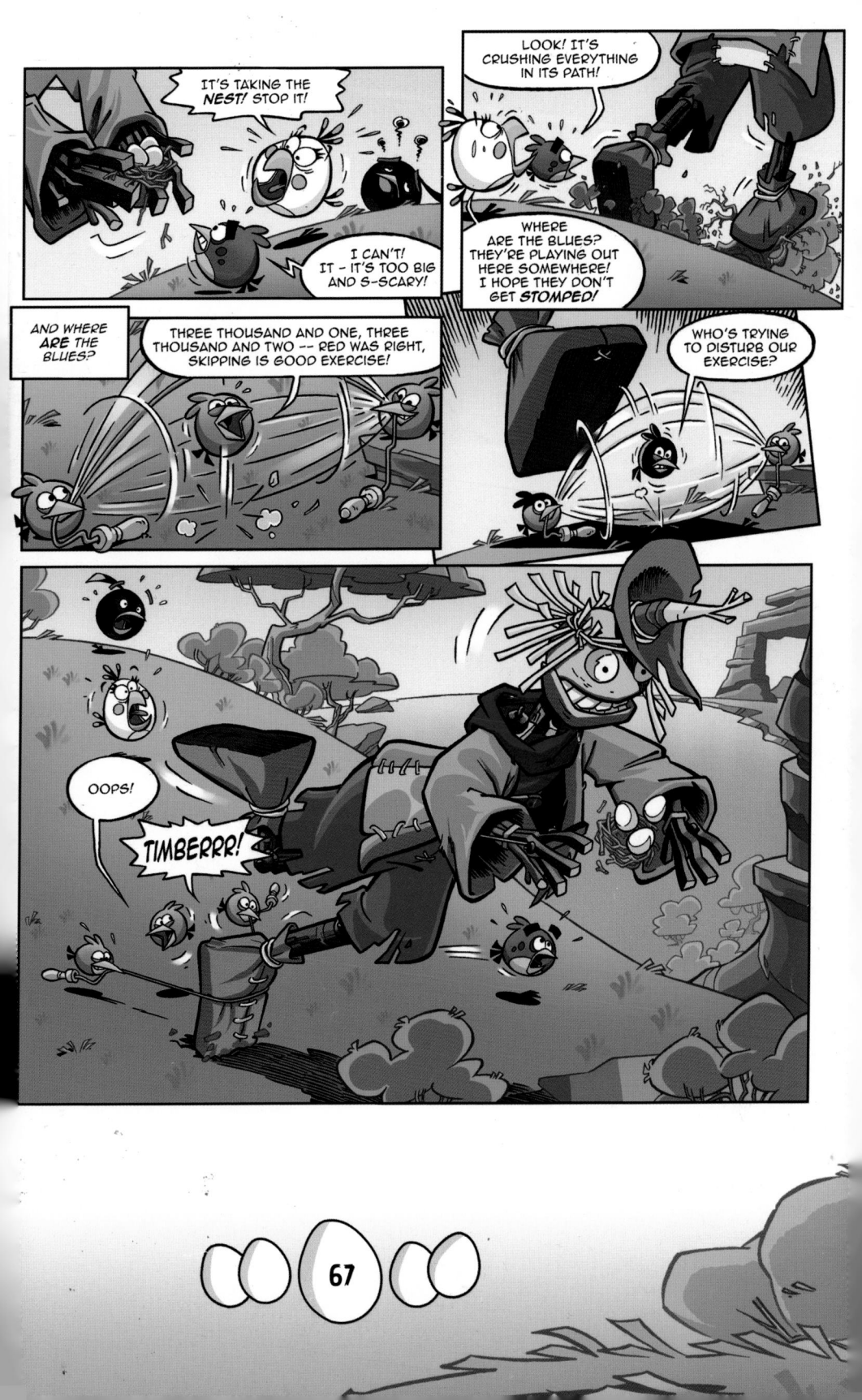
IT'S TAKING THE NEST! STOP IT!
I CAN'T! IT - IT'S TOO BIG AND S-SCARY!
LOOK! IT'S CRUSHING EVERYTHING IN ITS PATH!
WHERE ARE THE BLUES? THEY'RE PLAYING OUT HERE SOMEWHERE! I HOPE THEY DON'T GET STOMPED!
AND WHERE ARE THE BLUES?
THREE THOUSAND AND ONE, THREE THOUSAND AND TWO -- RED WAS RIGHT, SKIPPING IS GOOD EXERCISE!
WHO'S TRYING TO DISTURB OUR EXERCISE?
OOPS!
TIMBERRR!

I TOLD YOU SKIPPING WAS USEFUL!
KRUMMP!
RED -- DID YOU SAVE THE NEST?
YOU - YOU COULD SAY THAT!
IT - IT'S JUST A GIANT PUPPET - WITH PIGS IN IT!
DON'T HURT US! IT WASN'T OUR IDEA! WE - WE DIDN'T WANT TO BE A SCARECROW!
A SCARECROW? WE AREN'T CROWS YOU DOOFUS!
NOW THIS BROKEN HEAD REALLY DOES LOOK SCARY...
HMM... LET'S TEACH THOSE PIGS A LESSON...!

THAT NIGHT, AT THE PIG PALACE...
A LOVELY NIGHT FOR A STROLL ALONG THE BATTLEMENTS! I WONDER IF I'LL BE GETTING AN EGG SUPPER TONIGHT?
I'M SURE YOU WILL, YOUR MAJESTY!
SUDDENLY...
WOOOH! I AM THE ZOMBIE OF THE COBALT PLATEAU! I SMELL JUICY PIG FLESH! YUM!
HELLLP! ZOMBIE ATTACK!
RUN!
SAVE YOUR BACON!
EEK! OWCH!
AND...
NOW YOU KNOW WHAT IT'S LIKE BEING SCARED! YOU CAN HAVE YOUR SILLY TOY BACK NOW!
AND...
WELL AT LEAST IT HAS ONE MORE USE...
...GIVING YOU THE BOOT! UNTIL YOU CAN COME UP WITH SOMETHING BETTER!
OW! YES, YOUR HIGHNESS! EEK!
THE END

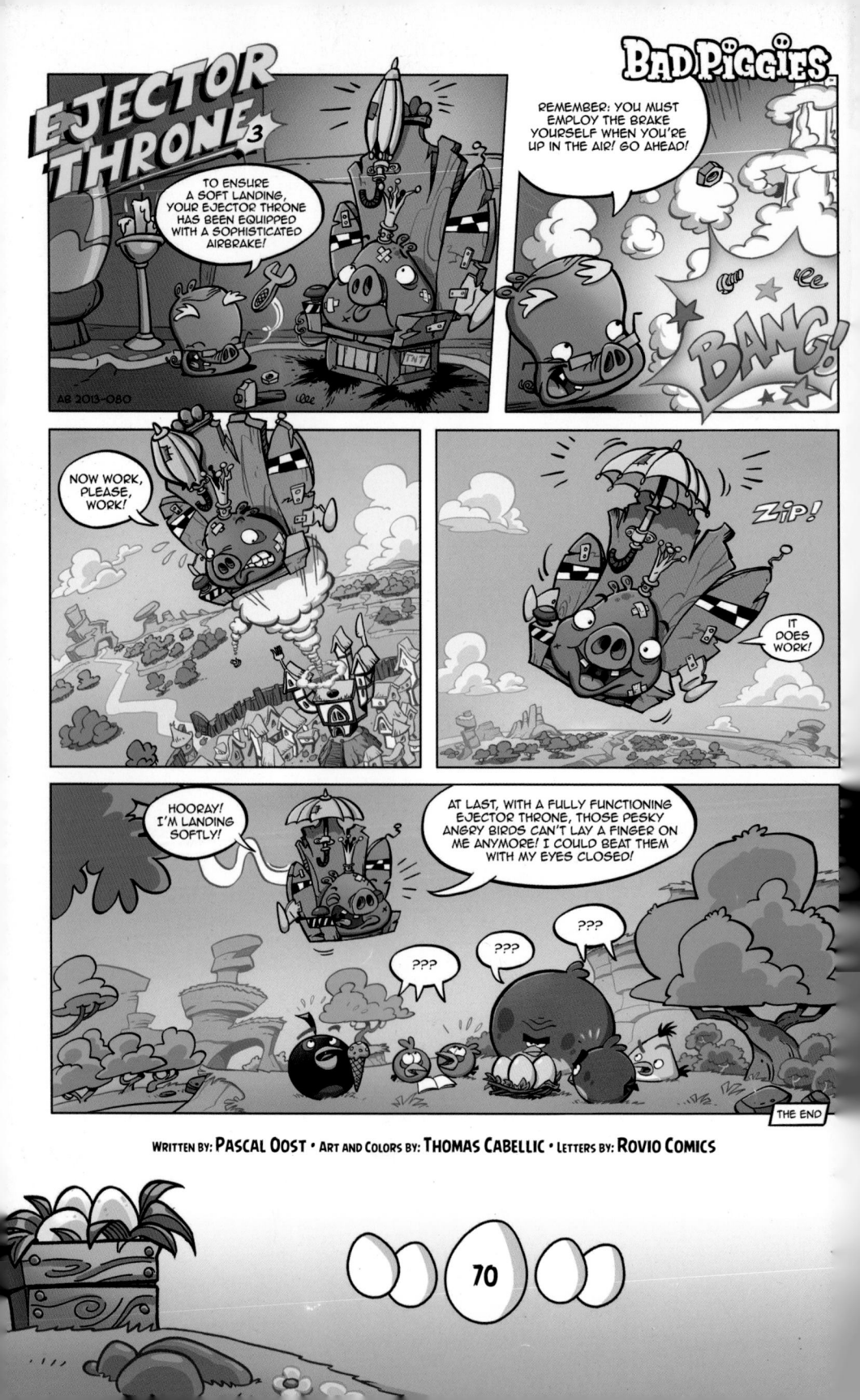

WRITTEN BY: PASCAL OOST • ART AND COLORS BY: THOMAS CABELLIC • LETTERS BY: ROVIO COMICS

IDW
PACHECO
ANGRY BIRDS
COMICS
BY: JORGE PACHECO
BY: DIEGO RODRIGUEZ

Artwork by: Ciro Cangialosi

Artwork by: Paco Rodrigues
Colors by: Digikore Studios

Artwork by: Ciro Cangialosi
2015

Concept by: UPL
Artwork by: Paco Rodriques

YOU'VE SEEN THE MOVIE, NOW SEE THE ART

THE MOST DOWNLOADED APP IN HISTORY IS NOW A MAJOR ANIMATED MOTION PICTURE, AND *THE ART OF THE ANGRY BIRDS MOVIE* SHOWCASES THE AMAZING ARTWORK THAT BRINGS THE FILM TO LIFE! SEE RED, CHUCK, BOMB, MATILDA, KING MUDBEARD, TERENCE, AND MIGHTY EAGLE, LIKE NEVER BEFORE!

HC • FC • 194 Pages • 12" x 9.5" • $39.99 • ISBN: 978-1-63140-604-1

© 2009 - 2016 Rovio Entertainment Ltd. and Rovio Animation Ltd. Rovio, Angry Birds, Bad Piggies, Might Eagle and all related properties, titles, logos and characters are trademarks of Rovio Entertainment ltd. and Rovio Animation Ltd. All Rights Reserved.

IDW KAIKEN PUBLISHING LTD. ROVI